THE
WITCH
WHO
LIVES
DOWN
THE
HALL

Written by
DONNA GUTHRIE

Illustrated by
AMY SCHWARTZ

HBJ

HARCOURT
BRACE
JOVANOVICH
PUBLISHERS

SAN DIEGO   NEW YORK   LONDON

THE
WITCH
WHO
LIVES
DOWN
THE
HALL

To my parents, Opal and Wally Winnett
— D. G.

To Laurel
— A. S.

Library of Congress Cataloging in Publication Data
Guthrie, Donna.
   The witch who lives down the hall.
   Summary: A young boy who lives in an apartment
house is convinced that his mysterious new neighbor
is a witch.
   1. Children's stories, American. [1. Witchcraft —
Fiction. 2. Neighborliness — Fiction. 3. Apartment
houses — Fiction] I. Schwartz, Amy, ill. II. Title.
PZ7.G9834Wi 1985   [E]   85-887
ISBN 0-15-298610-3

Designed by Dalia Hartman

Printed in the United States of America

First edition

A B C D E

This is my apartment building.
I live on the fourteenth floor with
my mother.
Our apartment building looks
like every other apartment building
in the city, but it isn't.

A witch lives down the hall from me.

Her name is Ms. McWee. She has long curly hair and big round glasses. She wears an old blue jogging suit and sneakers with yellow stripes. I admit she doesn't look like an average witch.

But witches sometimes wear disguises.

My mother thinks Ms. McWee is just a nice lady who lives with her cranky cat, Malcolm.

I'm not so sure.

For instance, the day we moved into our apartment, Ms. McWee said to my mother, "I'm so glad you have a little boy who's interested in astronomy, tropical fish, and books."

I think Ms. McWee looked into her crystal ball because she knew all about me before we met.

A witch can tell the future by gazing into a crystal ball.

My mother said, "Ms. McWee knows about your hobbies because she saw the moving men bring in a big blue telescope, a twenty-five gallon aquarium, and boxes and boxes of your books."

I'm not so sure.

Ms. McWee has strange friends who come to visit. They bring big books of magic and cases filled with magic charms.

Witches hold special meetings where they share their magic secrets.

My mother says, "Those people are members
of Ms. McWee's reading and music club. The cases
hold instruments, not charms, and the books are
about music, not magic." Mother also tells me
I should mind my own business.

I'm not so sure.

Late at night, I lie awake listening to Ms. McWee practicing her witchcraft. I hear the *click clack* of her magic beads all night long.

Witches practice their special noisy magic late at night.

My mother says that *click clack* noise is Ms. McWee's home computer and it's time to go to sleep.

I'm not so sure.

One Saturday morning, while my mother was
sleeping, I went outside to pick up the newspaper
in the hallway. The wind blew the apartment door
shut, and I was left alone in the hallway.

Suddenly, Ms. McWee appeared out of nowhere
and asked if she could help. I explained what
happened. Ms. McWee pulled a strand of long,
brown, curly hair from her head, and before I
could say "Hocus pocus," she turned the strand of
hair into some type of key that unlocked our door.

A witch has the power to change things.

My mother said, "Ms. McWee used one of her
bobby pins and jiggled the lock."

But I'm not so sure.

Once when I was sick, Ms. McWee brought over a mysterious potion. She said it was an old family recipe.

I just knew it was made of bat wings and spider legs. I didn't want to eat it because I was afraid it would make me feel worse. But I ate it anyway and I began to feel better.

A witch can stir up magic potions to make people well.

My mother said it was plain old chicken soup. But I'm not so sure.

Early one morning, I crept out onto the balcony with my blue telescope. I wanted to watch Ms. McWee performing magic. Soon I spied her. She was dressed in black, sitting on a magic carpet, singing an eerie song to her grumpy cat, Malcolm.

A witch uses a magic carpet if she doesn't have a broom. Witches also sing weird magic chants.

My mother said that Ms. McWee was wearing a leotard, sitting on an exercise mat, and doing her morning yoga.

She said that there's nothing magic about Ms. McWee, Malcolm, or yoga, and that I should use my telescope for stargazing, not spying.

I'm not so sure.

On Halloween, Ms. McWee's door was the only one in the whole building that was decorated. She pasted big orange pumpkins all over it, and hung a scary white ghost on the hall light.

Witches love Halloween.

My mother said, "Ms. McWee just likes to decorate for the holidays."

But I'm not so sure.

On Halloween night, I dressed up in my red devil suit and went trick-or-treating from door to door. Most people didn't even remember it was Halloween.

Miss Elliott, the ballet dancer who lives in 14C, didn't remember. She didn't have any candy so she gave me a health-food bar.

Mr. Crocket, the piano player who lives
in 14E, was having a party for grown-ups. He
didn't have any candy, either, so he gave me a
rye cracker with cheese spread on it.

But when I went to Ms. McWee's apartment, she
hadn't forgotten about Halloween. She was ready.

As I walked down the hall the door swung
open all by itself. The apartment was dark except
for one big smiling jack-o'-lantern. Ms. McWee had
on a long, black, witch's gown and a tall, pointed
hat. Malcolm wore an orange ribbon around his
neck and he seemed to be smiling at me.

She knew I was coming. The table was set for two.

We ate frosted pumpkin cookies and spiced apple tea by the light of her spooky jack-o'-lantern.

Ms. McWee said, "Do a trick for me."

So I stood on my head in the corner and whistled.

Then she gave me a treat—a bag of real candy!
Witches give the best Halloween parties.

This is our apartment building.

It looks like any other apartment building in the city, but it isn't.

Because Ms. McWee lives down the hall from me with her cranky cat, Malcolm.

Maybe she can't tell the future with a crystal ball or stir up potions to make people well.

Maybe she doesn't hold secret meetings or practice her witchcraft at night.

Maybe she doesn't have a flying carpet or the power to change things.

But there is something magical and mysterious about Ms. McWee.

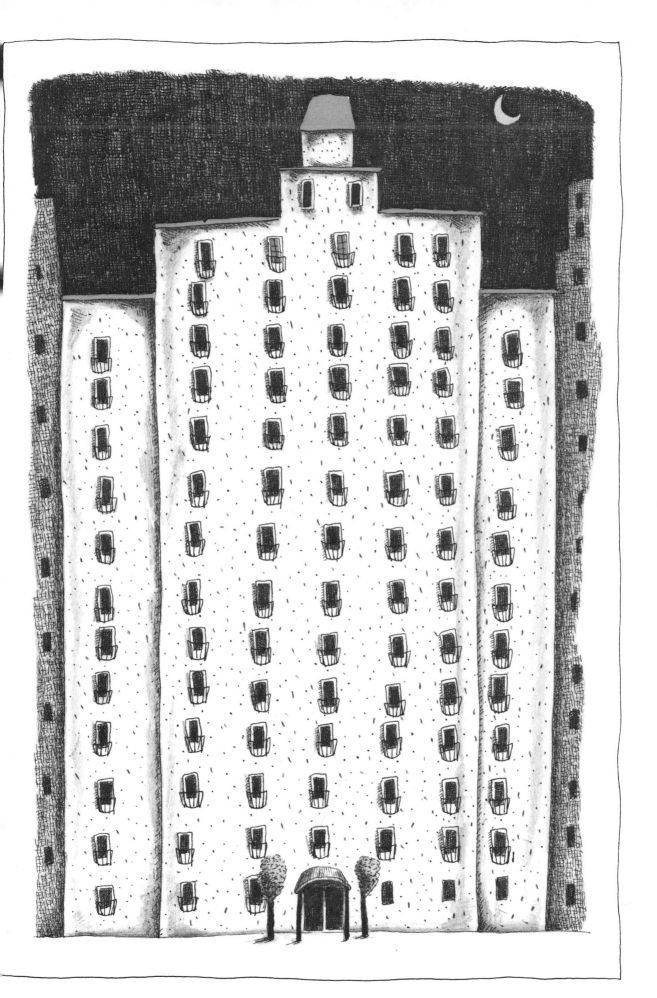

I'm sure of it!

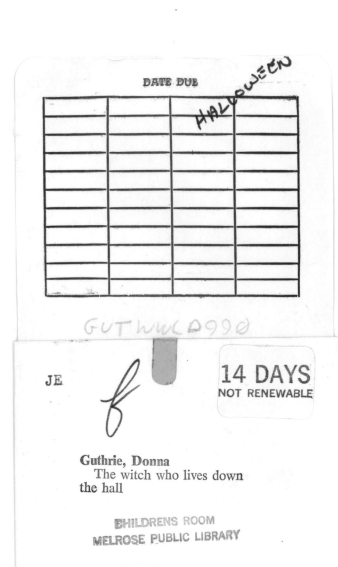